SOPHIE AND THE
TINY DOGNAPPING

A Book About Doing the Right Thing

Jamie Michalak · *Illustrated by* **Lorian Tu**

Charlesbridge

Welcome to 123 Sunshine Street,
home of five best friends who call themselves
the Sunshine Squad.

Together they do kind deeds and spread sunshine. They're everyday heroes. But as one of them is about to find out, even heroes need help sometimes. . . .

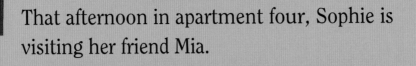

That afternoon in apartment four, Sophie is visiting her friend Mia.

"I wish I had a dollhouse like yours," Sophie says.

Mia's dollhouse has tiny furniture, dishes, and even working lights. But what Sophie loves most of all is its small dog. Sophie named her Emma.

Emma always smiles at Sophie with love.
We are meant to be together, Sophie thinks.

"I never even play with that dollhouse," Mia says.
"It was Abuela's." She leaps to the window.
"I'd rather play basketball. Let's go!"

Sophie gazes at Emma, snug in her hand.

She's so small, Sophie thinks. *Nobody will notice if I take her home. Besides, Mia doesn't even like dollhouses.*

Without a word, Sophie slips the dog into her pocket.

Back at home Sophie introduces Emma to her new family.

"This is Fuzzypants," says Sophie. "And Froggy, Rockhead, Tootsie, Lucy, Pepper . . .

Emma, do you know that there are five thousand kinds of frogs? Do you know a dog's sense of smell is a thousand times better than a human's?"

Emma stares at her with wide eyes.

She looks nervous, Sophie thinks.

"It's okay," says Sophie. "You'll feel at home soon."

That day, when Sophie gives
her pets food and water,
she also feeds Emma.

She gives her a bath

and tucks her into bed.

As she does, Sophie notices that her tummy feels funny. Playing with Emma doesn't feel the same as it did when she was at Mia's.

Sophie hasn't brought just Emma home. She's brought a bad feeling with her, too.

The next morning Sophie notices that
Emma looks like she misses her dollhouse.
Sophie wonders if Mia misses Emma, too.

Emma is small, but Sophie's secret feels big.
It follows her like a giant's shadow.

What have I done? Sophie thinks.
I need the Sunshine Squad's help.

Outside, Sophie joins her squad at their usual spot.
She is relieved to see that Mia isn't around yet.

"Hi, Sophie," Lucas says. "Why did the lemon cry?"

"I don't know. Why?" Sophie asks.

"Because the banana split!" he replies. "Get it? *Orange* you glad I told that joke?"

Tommy laughs, but Sophie is too nervous to even smile.

"I have a serious question," she says. "Is it okay to take something that doesn't belong to you if it's very small?"

"No," says Oliver. "Heroes know wrong is wrong, no matter what size it is."

"Yup," Lucas agrees. "Small can still be trouble. Like this small fly in Tommy's lemonade."

Plop!

"Ew," says Tommy.

"Or this small ink blotch on Oliver's shirt."

Squirt!

"Hey!" says Oliver.

"Even a small hole in a water balloon can lead to—"

SPLASH!

"A big mess!" cries Tommy.

"I get it," says Sophie.

"The plastic fly?" says Lucas.
"Great! That will be ten cents."

"No, I get what I need to do," says Sophie.

But doing it might mean she'll get in trouble.
And what if Mia won't be her friend anymore?

Just then, Mia appears. And so does Sophie's
bad feeling. *I'm SCARED*, Sophie thinks.
Gathering her courage, she turns to Mia . . .

"I took your dollhouse's dog. I'm sorry," Sophie says.

As she hands Mia's dog back, something funny happens—
the bad feeling in her tummy begins to disappear.

"Oh," says Mia quietly.

She looks at her dog. Then she looks at Sophie . . .

"Thank you for giving her back," Mia says. "That was brave."

Sophie asks, "So you're still my friend?"

"Of course. Everyone makes mistakes," says Mia. "I accidentally broke my brother's model plane once. I felt awful. The only way to fix it was with the truth."

"And *lots* of glue," says Lucas.

"Speaking of lots," says Oliver, "look how much sunshine we've spread today! Who wants to make more lemonade?"

"I will," says Sophie. "But first I need to do something."

"Bye, Emma," says Sophie, smiling at her.

And Emma smiles back.

Start with the Truth

It was a beautiful sunny day, and Mary and I were playing in her new basement because it was so hot outside. The two of us were best friends, so we naturally did what best friends do—we did everything together. We went camping together, we trusted each other, and always stuck up for each other.

But that day, something changed.

I'll never forget the look on Mary's face when she knocked over her mother's favorite vase that was on the table. The flowers and vase crashed to the floor, and the vase cracked into tons of tiny little pieces. I looked at Mary and said, "There's no way to fix this!"

Mary burst into tears. "What am I going to do? What am I going to say?" She looked at me while she wiped her tears and asked, "Can you say that you did it?"

I was shocked. I didn't know what to do or say, and I started to pace back and forth.

"Okay, I'll do it," I said.

That very second, her mother came downstairs to ask about the loud noise she had just heard. Mary said, "Mom, we were sitting on the couch, and Michelle put her feet on the table and knocked over the vase."

Her mother looked at me and shook her head. "I don't know how many times I have to tell you girls, you don't put your feet on the table."

I apologized to Mary's mother and told her I would buy her a new vase. She said not to worry—but to just be more careful. I felt so bad—and I didn't even do it! I knew that I had kept Mary out of trouble, but I also felt that it wasn't right.

I didn't go over to Mary's for a few days, and she didn't come to my house, either. I was busy cleaning and doing extra chores. Finally, I earned enough money to buy Mary's mother a new vase. I shopped around for a vase that looked like the one that Mary had broken until I found one that I thought her mom would like. Wanting to get it over with, I went straight to Mary's house to give her mom the new vase. When Mary saw the vase that I had worked so hard to buy, she burst into tears again.

"Mom, I have to tell you something. I broke the vase, not Michelle," she confessed. "I asked her to take the blame for me."

Mary and I looked at each other with relief. Now I knew that Mary felt it was wrong to lie about the vase, too. Mary's mother had a talk with us about the importance of telling the truth from the beginning. Then Mary decided that she should do something to make things right with her mother and me. She asked if she would take us to the store, where Mary picked out some beautiful flowers for her mom's new vase and a pretty friendship bracelet for me. And she paid for them herself with her allowance.

—Michelle Rossi

Start Your Own Sunshine Squad!

Want to form your own Sunshine Squad of everyday heroes? Here's what to do:

1. Ask friends to be members.

2. Find a headquarters. It can be a stoop, a tree house, your bedroom, or anywhere you'd like! (Secret passwords are optional.)

3. Think of ways to spread sunshine in your own families, neighborhoods, and schools.

4. Add some fun! Make up nicknames for one another, a special squad handshake, or even a theme song.

5. Take the Sunshine Squad pledge:

   I, [say your name here], promise to make the world a better place by helping others, being thoughtful, and spreading sunshine to those I meet. Because even the smallest act of kindness can make someone's day!

For E. & S. Young—J. M.

For Lisa, who is still my best friend—and always will be.
And for Kerri, who always does the right thing.—L. T.

Text copyright © 2021 by Charlesbridge
Illustrations copyright © 2021 by Lorian Tu
Copyright © 2021 Chicken Soup for the Soul Editorial, LLC. All rights reserved.
CSS, Chicken Soup for the Soul, and its Logo and Marks are trademarks of Chicken Soup for the Soul, LLC.
All rights reserved, including the right of reproduction in whole or in part in any form.
Charlesbridge and colophon are registered trademarks of Charlesbridge Publishing, Inc.

At the time of publication, all URLs printed in this book were accurate and active. Charlesbridge,
the author, and the illustrator are not responsible for the content or accessibility of any website.

Published by Charlesbridge
9 Galen Street
Watertown, MA 02472
(617) 926-0329
www.charlesbridge.com

Library of Congress Cataloging-in-Publication Data
Names: Michalak, Jamie, author. | Tu, Lorian, illustrator.
Title: Sophie and the tiny dognapping: a book about doing the right thing / Jamie Michalak;
    illustrated by Lorian Tu.
Description: Watertown, MA: Charlesbridge, [2021] | Series: Chicken soup for the soul kids |
    Audience: Ages 4–7. | Audience: Grades K–1. | Summary: Sophie loves her friend Mia's elaborate
    dollhouse, especially the tiny dog, and since Mia does not even play with the dollhouse, Sophie
    thinks that nobody will notice if she takes the toy dog home with her—but afterward she feels guilty,
    and the rest of her friends at 123 Sunshine Street explain to her that what she did was wrong and help
    her to do the right thing.
Identifiers: LCCN 2020055548 (print) | LCCN 2020055549 (ebook) | ISBN 9781623542757 (hardcover) |
    ISBN 9781632898944 (ebook)
Subjects: LCSH: Theft—Juvenile fiction. | Dolls—Juvenile fiction. | Conduct of life—Juvenile fiction. |
    Best friends—Juvenile fiction. | CYAC: Stealing—Fiction. | Dolls—Fiction. | Conduct of life—Fiction. |
    Best friends—Fiction. | Friendship—Fiction.
Classification: LCC PZ7.W58453 Sop 2021 (print) | LCC PZ7.W58453 (ebook) | DDC [E]—dc23
LC record available at https://lccn.loc.gov/2020055548
LC ebook record available at https://lccn.loc.gov/2020055549

Printed in China
(hc) 10 9 8 7 6 5 4 3 2 1

Illustrations created digitally
Display type set in Midnight Chalker by Hanoded
Text type set in Oxford by Roger White
Color separations and printing by 1010 Printing International Limited in Huizhou, Guangdong, China
Production supervision by Jennifer Most Delaney
Designed by Kristen Nobles